GOO

For my friend Gina and her tiny plunger

Henry Holt and Company, *Publishers since 1866*
Henry Holt® is a registered trademark of Macmillan Publishing Group, LLC
120 Broadway, New York, NY 10271 • mackids.com

Our books may be purchased in bulk for promotional, educational, or business use.
Please contact your local bookseller or the Macmillan Corporate and Premium Sales Department
at (800) 221-7945 ext. 5442 or by email at MacmillanSpecialMarkets@macmillan.com.

Library of Congress Cataloging-in-Publication Data

Names: Mack, Jeff, author, illustrator.
Title: Marcel's masterpiece : how a toilet shaped the history of art / by Jeff Mack.
Description: New York : Henry Holt Books for Young Readers, 2022. |
Includes bibliographical references. | Audience: Ages 4-8. | Audience:
Grades 2-3. | Summary: Describes how artist Marcel Duchamp turned a
toilet into a famous work of art.
Identifiers: LCCN 2021046006 | ISBN 9781250777164 (hardcover)
Subjects: CYAC: Duchamp, Marcel, 1887-1968—Fiction. | Artists—Fiction.
Classification: LCC PZ7.M18973 Mar 2022 | DDC [E]--dc23
LC record available at https://lccn.loc.gov/2021046006

First edition, 2022
Book design by Cindy De la Cruz
The art for this book was created with acrylic and watercolor paint,
digital "ink," torn paper, cardboard, fabric, tape, string, wooden boxes,
cotton balls, and whatever else I could find around the house.
Printed in China by RR Donnelley Asia Printing Solutions Ltd.,
Dongguan City, Guangdong Province.

ISBN 978-1-250-77716-4 (hardcover)

1 3 5 7 9 10 8 6 4 2

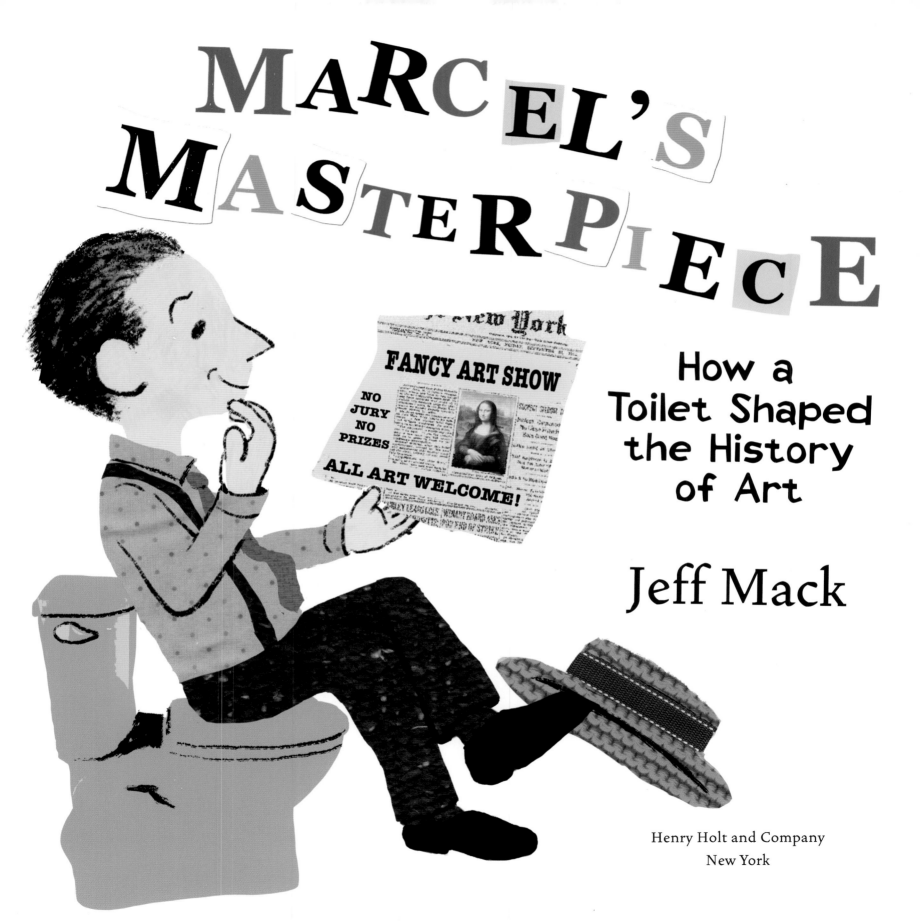

MaRCEL'S MASTERPIECE

How a Toilet Shaped the History of Art

FANCY ART SHOW

NO JURY NO PRIZES

ALL ART WELCOME!

Jeff Mack

Henry Holt and Company
New York

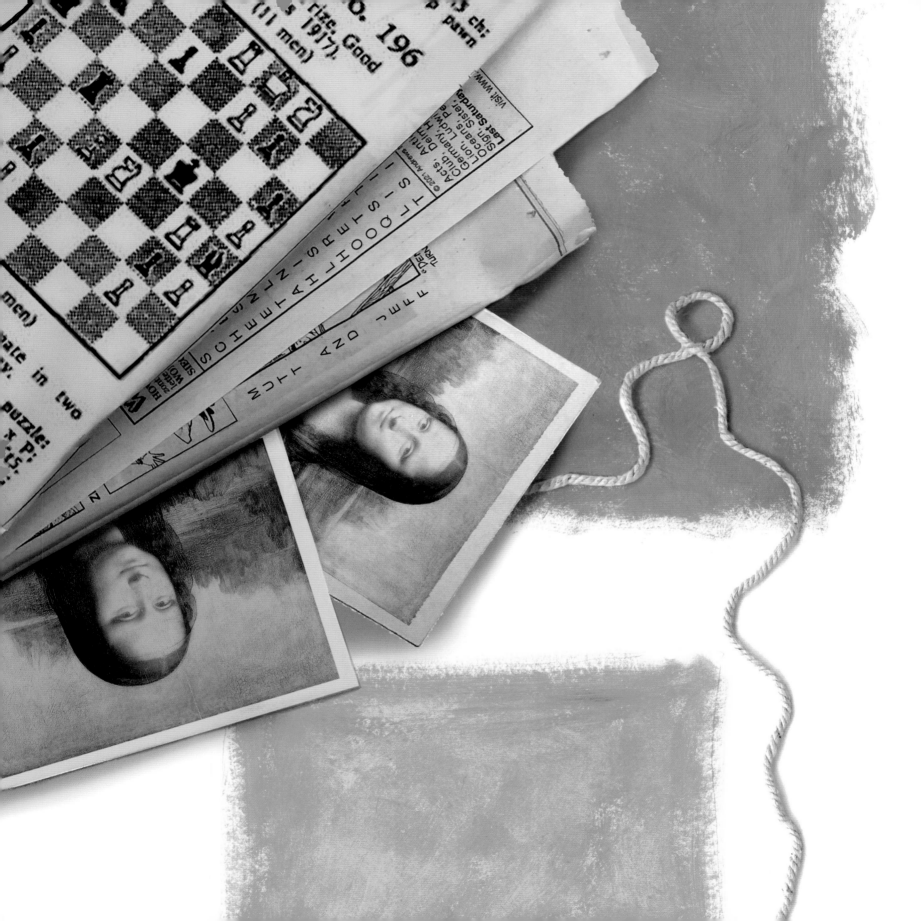

He shaved a star into

the back of his hair.

I MEANT TO DO THAT.

He bought it.
DO YOU WANT A PLUMBER TO HOOK THAT UP FOR YOU?
AND FLUSH ALL MY HARD WORK DOWN THE DRAIN?

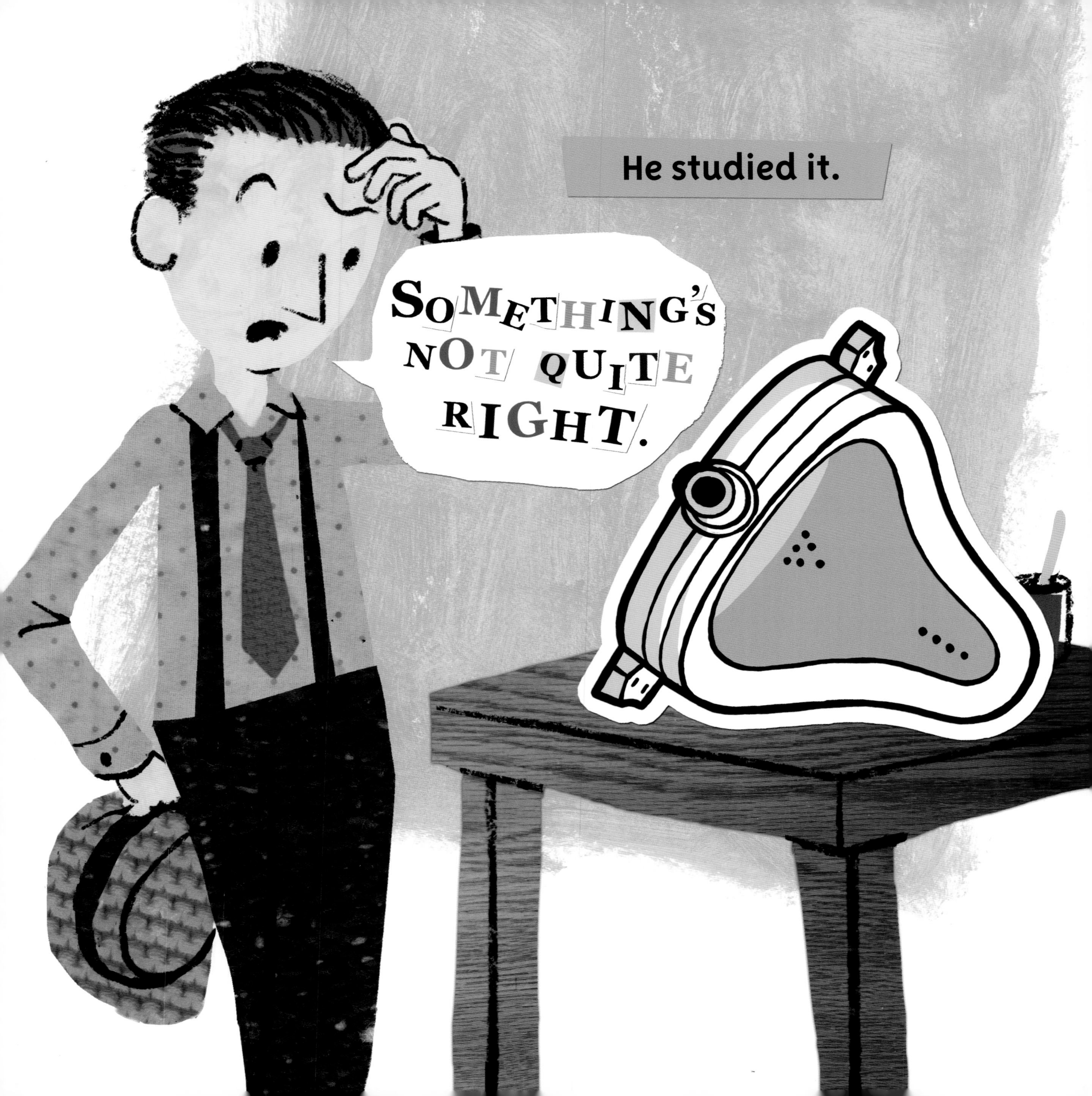
He studied it.
SOMETHING'S NOT QUITE RIGHT.

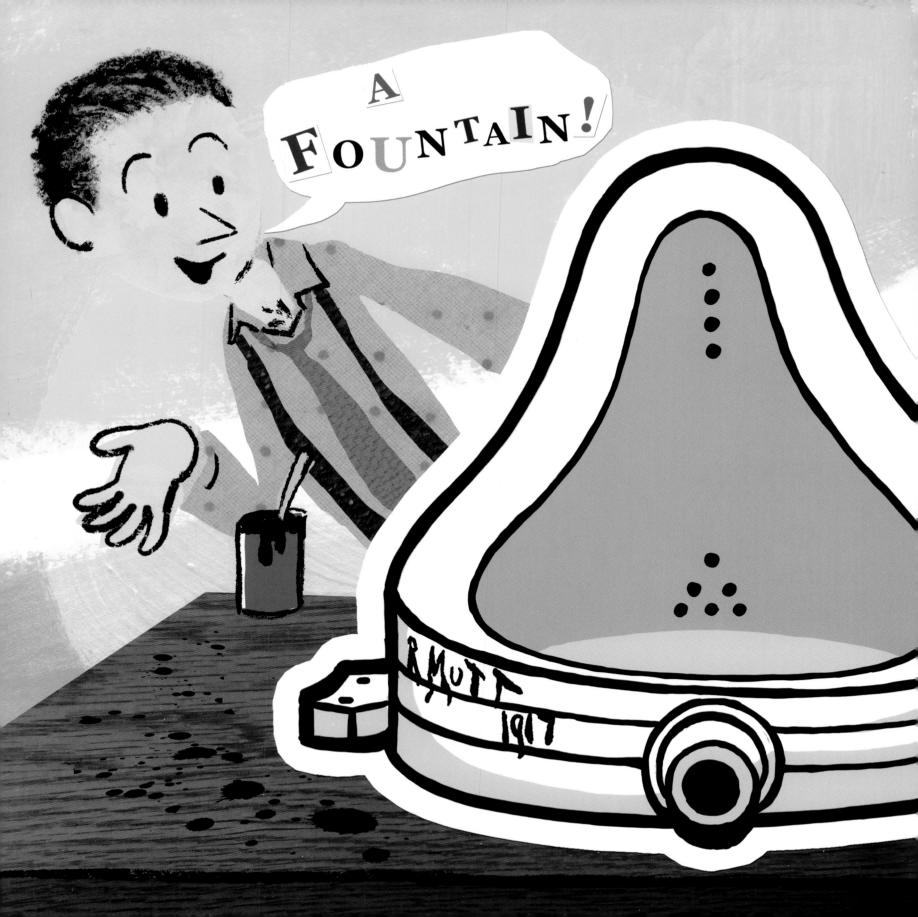

A friend took it.

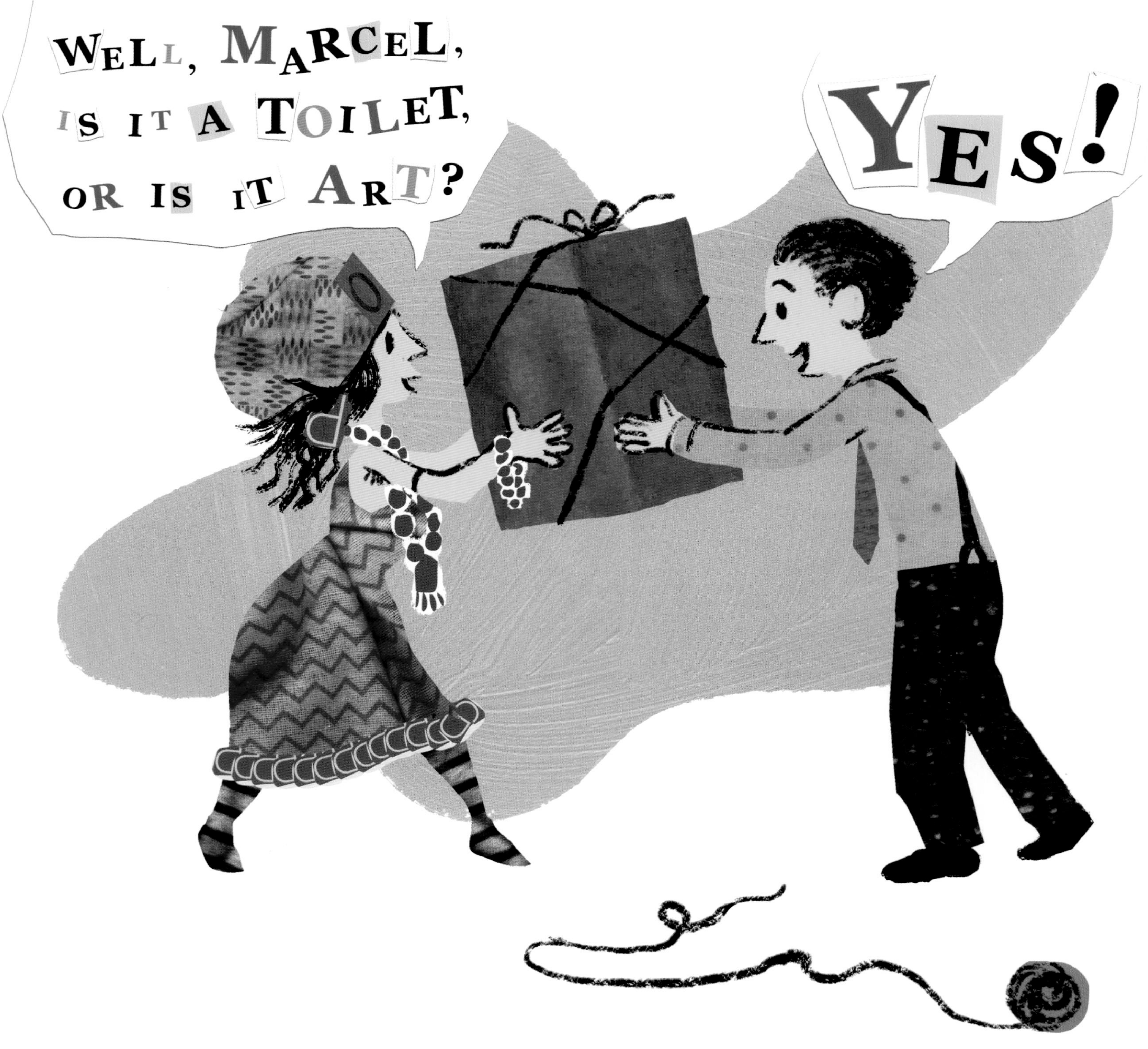

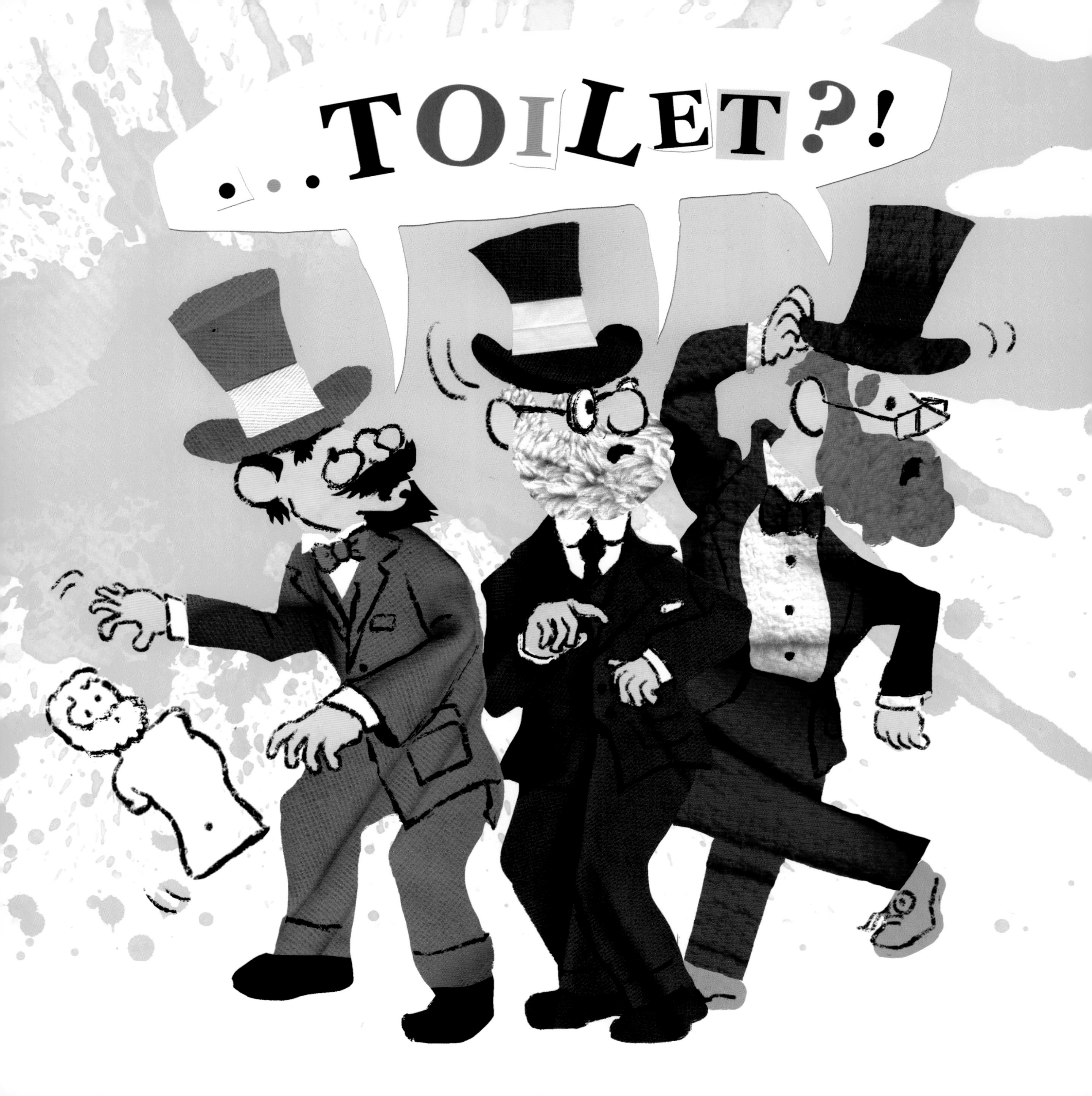
...TOILET?!

They saw it.

They argued about it.
A TOILET IS NOT REALLY ART. I WILL NOT LET YOU GO!
I SAY IT IS ART! AND I REALLY NEED TO GO BAD!

In 1917, Marcel's *Fountain* made

quite a splash.

WELL, IT DID GET PEOPLE TO THINK ABOUT ART, DIDN'T IT?

MARCEL DUCHAMP AND HIS DADA

Marcel Duchamp was a painter from France. When he moved to New York City in 1915, he stopped painting so he could try something new.

I REALLY SHOULD TRY SOMETHING NEW.

"I was interested in ideas," he said.

He started to shape his ideas into art the way some artists shape a lump of clay into sculpture.

Marcel thought having a good idea was the most important part of art, even more important than how the art looked.

To prove it, he chose ordinary objects like a stool and a bicycle wheel. He put them together and called them art.

It was even easier with the urinal. By turning it upside down, changing its name to *Fountain*, and putting it in an art show, Marcel changed the way people thought about it. Sure, it was the same urinal, but it no longer *worked* like a urinal.

It had a new purpose: **ART!**

Can a toilet really be art? Maybe the *real* art was Marcel's idea to call it art.

Anything is art if an artist says it is.

Marcel called these objects "readymades." They didn't look exciting, but they changed the way people thought about art.

Until then, most people thought art meant only beautiful paintings and sculptures that were made by hand. When they saw Duchamp's readymades, they had to ask themselves:

WHY?   and also: WHY NOT?

If his readymades were art, what else could be art?

HMM...

Andy Warhol in 1962

For example, sometimes Marcel pretended to be an imaginary person named Rrose Sélavy. Rrose wore makeup and a fur coat.

He noticed that people were often friendlier to Rrose than they were to Marcel.

MARCEL? WHO'S MARCEL?

GET OUT OF MY WAY!

HEY!

THEY SMILED AND OPENED DOORS FOR RROSE.

AFTER YOU.

MY, WHAT A GENTLEMAN!

Did Marcel change who he *really* was just by changing his clothes? Or did he simply change the way people *thought* of him?

Was pretending to be someone else also a type of art?

Art like Marcel's was called **DADA**!

Hannah Höch and
Kurt Schwitters

DADA!

Yes, it was a silly word that sounded like baby talk, but Dada artists had a serious goal. They wanted to show people that there were many different ways to make fun and interesting art with readymades. So they cut up magazines and used the pieces to make new pictures called collages.

They chose random words from the dictionary and wrote funny nonsense poems. Sometimes they even made up their own words.

. . . Gaga Di Bling Blong Gaga Blong!

Hugo Ball

DING!

BCDEFGHIJKLM
NOPQRSTUVWXYZ

They built their own costumes and instruments from household objects and made music that sounded like nothing anyone had ever heard before.

Dee Doo Doo Doo Dee Dada Daaaaaa!

Artists have been using readymades ever since.

In 1942, Pablo Picasso made a bull's head by combining a bicycle seat and handlebars.

Baroness Elsa von Freytag-Loringhoven

TA-DA!

In 1961, John Cage performed four minutes and thirty-three seconds of silence.

squeak.

For him, the random coughs from the audience and the sounds of their squeaky chairs were all part of his music.

Can noises be readymades, too?

In 1971, Yoko Ono added one letter to the . . .

Museum Of Modern art

After that, who could think of the famous museum in the same way?

F

In 2019, Maurizio Cattelan taped a banana to the wall of his art gallery and called it *Comedian.* It sold for $120,000! So what did the collector really buy? The banana or the idea?

BUT WHY, MAURIZIO? WHY?

IT'S GOT A PEEL.

Today, more than one hundred years after Marcel's *Fountain*, people still argue about art.

How can we tell when something is art or when it isn't?

WHO GETS TO DECIDE?

And most importantly, what ideas help us think about our world in new and interesting ways?

??????

MAMA

DADA